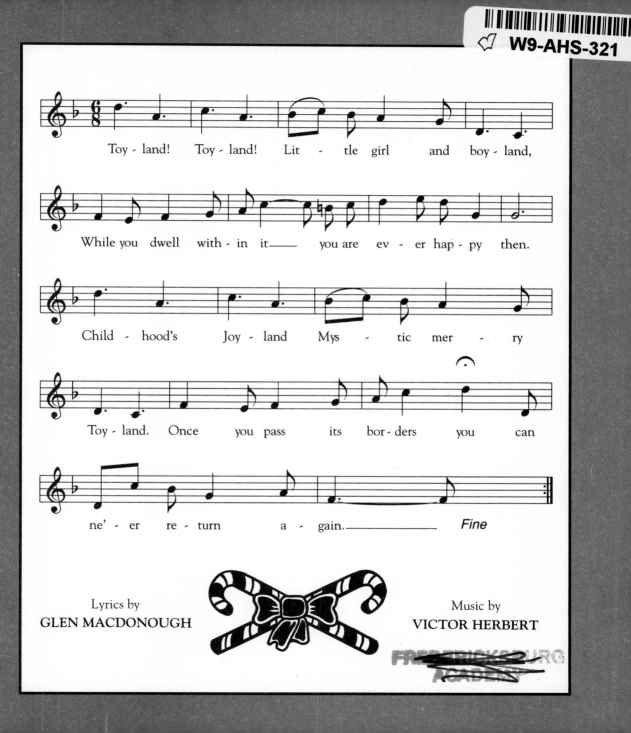

Toy - land! Toy - land! Lit - tle girl and boy - land,

While you dwell with - in it___ you are ev - er hap - py then.

Child - hood's Joy - land Mys - tic mer - ry

Toy - land. Once you pass its bor - ders you can

ne' - er re - turn a - gain.___ *Fine*

Lyrics by
GLEN MACDONOUGH

Music by
VICTOR HERBERT

W9-AHS-321

FREDERICKSBURG ACADEMY

FIC
McD

Woodruff Gift

$5.95

3-21-94

94- 1904

MARCH OF THE WOODEN SOLDIERS

Based On The 1903 Musical
By Victor Herbert And
Glen MacDonough

Illustrated By
VICTORIA LISI

As Told By
Mandi McDonald

The Unicorn Publishing House, Inc.
Morris Plains, New Jersey

March of the Wooden Soldiers

 ome close and listen, and I'll tell you a tale,
Of fourteen children you know very well.
Off in Mother Goose Land far, far away
The Widow Piper's children play through the day.

"A party! A party!" they would all shout.
"Pass the sweet cakes, pass the cider, please all about!
"A party! A party!" they would all say.
"Come, join in the fun the live long day!"

But someone soon came to ruin their fun.
Wicked old Barnaby—that is the one.
"Chase him away! Chase him away!
"He'll RUIN our party! He'll RUIN the day!"

March of the Wooden Soldiers

And old miser Barnaby soon ran away
Cursing the children, "Someday they'll pay!"
He called for his henchmen—a villianous lot.
"There is trouble to cause; there is mischief to PLOT!"

But the villians had other things to do at the time.
To woo Widow Piper was chief on their minds.
"Tell us pretty maid," they said with a smile,
"Can we come in—come in for a while?"

March of the Wooden Soldiers

Ah, but Tom Tom, the widow's elder son,
Knew how to end their villianous fun.
With a WHACK! on one bottom and a WHACK! on another,
He soon sent them scurrying—running for cover.

March of the Wooden Soldiers

Old Barnaby came calling at the next hour,
With a sly little grin and a bouquet of flowers.
"Mary, my sweet," he called from the door,
"Come out and see the one you adore."

"Pooh!" said Mary, "you WICKED old man,
"I'm to marry your nephew—just as fast as I can."
"That good-for-nothing Alan!" Barnaby cried.
"That boy has always been a thorn in my side!"

Mary then took the heel of her shoe
And stomped with one foot—then the other one too.
Barnaby let out such a howl and a scream
That EVEN Sleeping Beauty would wake from her dream.

March of the Wooden Soldiers

But when Alan arrived trouble soon came,
For the flowers were left with Barnaby's name.
Mary pleaded and begged it just wasn't true,
"I never loved Barnaby—I have only LOVED you!"

The young lovers soon began to bicker and fight,
Each one believing they're in the right.
"Don't you ever speak to me!" Mary cried out.
And with a sob and a wail she ran in the house.

Now when Barnaby heard of their fight,
He gathered his henchmen well out of sight.
An evil plan grew clear in his mind.
"Nothing will stop me—stop me this TIME!"

"I will rid myself of those bothersome brats,
"With one deliciously despicable act.
"You will take my niece, Jane, and my nephew, too,
"Into the Spider's Forest where both you will lose."

"I told them of a house where they would both live,
"And said their inheritance I would gladly give
"If they would but go through the forest this night.
"The Spider will get them or they'll BOTH die of fright!"

March of the Wooden Soldiers

"Goodbye, goodbye!" Barnaby called out.
"That's the last I'll see of you two no doubt."
So deep into the Spider's Forest they did go—
A murky wet wood where cold winds blow.

And it wasn't long before the villians snuck away,
Leaving the children lost for their way.
Night fell fast as the children wandered blind
While glowing EVIL eyes peered from EVERY side.

Lost and weary the children lay down
And soon were asleep on the soft ground.
Fairies of the Wood pleaded and screamed,
"Wake up, children, wake up from your dreams!"

March of the Wooden Soldiers

But Fairy voices sound to us like the wind,
So as the children sleep on, the Spider begins,
To weave a deadly web above their dear heads:
Filling every Fairy's heart with loathing and dread.

"Help us, Great Bear!" they called at the cave.
"The Spider is coming, the children MUST be saved!"
In the next moment, a Great Bear appeared—
All claws and teeth even Dread Spider feared.

The Spider flew furiously back up its web,
As hundreds of Fairies lifted them and fled.
Far from the Forest they set the two down.
At the gates of Toyland they would be found.

March of the Wooden Soldiers

Toyland is by far a magical town
Where every toy imagined can surely be found.
A place beyond the sweetest of dreams
Where nothing is ever quite what it seems.

March of the Wooden Soldiers

Now, Mary to Toyland had fled by this time.
Old Barnaby's words, "You SHALL be mine!"
Had scared the poor child beyond all compare,
"I'll never go home! On this I do swear!"

But Barnaby was clever—clever as could be,
"She might fool some, but she'll never FOOL me!"
Off with Widow Piper to Toyland he hurried
To hire a Detective and flush out his quarry.

March of the Wooden Soldiers

The Widow Piper's children came for the fun.
Off to the Toyshop in a fast run!
Where the Toymaker greeted all with a smile,
"Come in, my dear children, come in for a while."

At once, the children came fast down the stairs
And caught the Toymaker quite unprepared.
They grabbed him by the arms and shouted with glee,
"Show us your toyshop, oh please, let us SEE!"

March of the Wooden Soldiers

After the children had seen all the toys
They hurried away with joyful noise.
As Barnaby snuck in to speak wicked words—
The most wicked the Toymaker had ever, EVER heard.

"I wish you to make toys that have never been made.
"Toys that can hurt, can injure, can maim!
"Toys that will kick, and will pinch, and will bite;
"Sending the children screaming in fright."

"Never, Never, NEVER!" the Toymaker cried.
"Before I would do that I would surely die.
"Why, I have even caught all the evil that abounds
"Bottled it away—see here—safe and sound."

March of the Wooden Soldiers

Barnaby went away knowing just what to do,
But of one thing he had never a clue.
That Alan and Jane were still both alive
Having hid at the Toyshop in clever disguise.

But Mary wasn't fooled, when first she arrived,
"Alan, my love, it is YOU!" she cried.
"Shhhh!" Alan said, "Barnaby might hear.
"Oh please, Mary, forgive, forgive me my dear."

March of the Wooden Soldiers

And Alan and Mary hugged through the night
Till morning's first rays cast out their light.
The day of the Christmas Parade had come at last:
The PARADE OF THE TOYS with pageantry passed.

The Parade was by far beyond all compare
With soldiers, ballerinas, and fat teddy bears.
The people were gathered all along the way
To cheer the new toys with a smile and a wave.

March of the Wooden Soldiers

While Toyland was gathered to see the toys off
Barnaby crept quietly for the evil he sought.
In the Toyshop he found a bottle marked 'DANGER!'
"Ah-ha! Here's some fun for a wicked old stranger!"

Releasing the evil on the toys that were left
"Rise, army of fiends—rise at my request!"
But evil knows no master: having its own wicked ways
"Obey me," screamed Barnaby, "obey me I say!"

At that very moment the Toymaker came back
And as evil hates good—it was HIM they attacked!
"Oh, my beautiful toys! What has he done?
"Where once was love, now there is none."

March of the Wooden Soldiers

By the time Alan came the evil had fled
"I can't believe my eyes," Barnaby said.
"You're still alive, well, I'll soon change that!
"You, my dear boy, are like a mouse in a trap!"

Now Alan didn't try to run or to hide
But went straight away to the Toymaker's side.
As Barnaby called to the crowd gathered near,
"He has killed the Toymaker—killed him I fear."

The Toymaker still lived, but his sadness was deep.
He lay in dark slumber—a sinister sleep.
Alan was taken to the court to be tried.
The verdict came quickly: Alan must DIE.

March of the Wooden Soldiers

"Please, Alan's innocent, help him," she begged.
"Forget him, my dear, it is I you shall wed.
"So let nothing trouble that pretty little head
"For tomorrow, my child, Alan is DEAD!"

March of the Wooden Soldiers

The hanging was set for the very next day
No matter how Mary pleaded and prayed.
What could she do? What could she say?
To save her dear Alan from hanging that day.

Mary went to the Toymaker still fast asleep
And offered a prayer as a tear crossed her cheek,
"Please, dear Toymaker, don't let him die!
"Please wake from your dream. Oh, try, please, TRY!"

And as a tear rolled gently off Mary's cheek
The Toymaker slowly stirred from his sleep.
"I hear you, dear child, my sadness has passed.
"When there is love such as yours—goodness will last."

March of the Wooden Soldiers

The Toymaker then called the people together
"This boy is not a villian. Oh no, not EVER!
"Barnaby is the man whose evil has harmed.
"Find the wicked fellow. Sound the alarm!"

Old Barnaby was caught and thrown into jail
And once again in Toyland all was quite well.
The Toymaker called to all that might hear:
"Keep LOVE in your heart—hold LOVE always dear."

© 1992 The Unicorn Publishing House. All Rights Reserved
Artwork © 1990 Victoria Lisi. All Rights Reserved
Text © 1992 The Unicorn Publishing House. All Rights Reserved
This book may not be reproduced in whole or in part, by any means, with-
out written permission. For information, contact: Jean L. Scrocco, Unicorn
Publishing House, 120 American Road, Morris Plains, NJ 07950
Printed in U.S.A.

Printing History 15 14 13 12 11 10 9 8 7 6 5 4 3 2 1

This book is dedicated to
the children of the world
who believe in dreams.

Toyland